PAPER BOATS

PAPER BOATS

BY
Rabindranath Tagore

ILLUSTRATED BY
Grayce Bochak

CAROLINE HOUSE

Paper Boats, a selection from *Crescent Moon,* was originally printed in
Collected Poems and Plays by Rabindranath Tagore. Copyright 1913
by Macmillan Publishing Co., Inc., renewed 1914 by Rabindranath
Tagore.

Illustrations copyright © 1992 by Grayce Bochak

Published by Caroline House

Boyds Mills Press, Inc.
A Highlights Company
910 Church Street
Honesdale, Pennsylvania 18431

Publisher Cataloging-in-Publication Data

Tagore, Rabindranath, 1861-1941.
     Paper Boats / by Rabindranath Tagore ; illustrated by Grayce Bochak.
32p. : ill. ; cm.
Originally printed in Collected Poems and Plays by Rabindranath Tagore,
Macmillan Publishing Company, Inc., 1913.
Summary: A child launches paper boats hoping someone in another country will
find them.
ISBN 1-878093-12-6.
1. Children's poetry. 2. Picture-books. I. Bochak, Grayce, illus. II. Title.
891 /.44-dc20   [E]   1992
LC Card number : 91-72987

First edition, 1992

Type design by Charlotte Staub

Distributed by St. Martin's Press

Printed in the United States of America

For John

Day by day

I float my paper boats one by one,

Down the running stream,

In big black letters I write my name on them and the name of the village where I live.

I hope that someone in some strange land will find them and know who I am.

I load my little boats with shiuli flowers
from our garden, and hope that
these blooms of dawn will be
carried safely to land in the night.

I launch my paper boats

and look up
into the sky and see the little clouds
setting their white bulging sails.

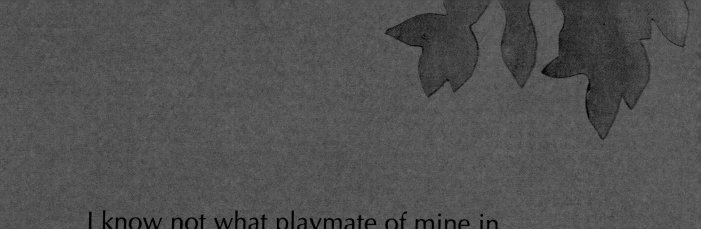

I know not what playmate of mine in
the sky sends them down the air to
race with my boats!

When night comes I bury my face in my arms

and dream that my paper boats float on and on
under the midnight stars.

The fairies of sleep are sailing in them,
and the lading is their baskets

full of dreams.